# SKELETON WOMAN

By ALBERTO VILLOLDO    Illustrated by YOSHI

There was no warning of the tsunami. The giant wave came thundering from the sea, wrecking the ice houses, smashing the boats and the dogsleds, crushing everything in its path.

After the storm, the villagers searched for their friends and relatives and discovered that the only one missing was Annuk.

Annuk was strong and fast like the wind. Her
bright eyes sparkled when she whipped across the
snow on her sled, or when she tracked the wild
wolf dogs in the forest.

Now the sea had taken her.

The villagers built a great fire in the roundhouse and sang sad songs, praying that the king of the sea take care of Annuk, wherever she may be. But Annuk could not hear the songs. She could not hear her sled dogs crying in the night or the *boom-boom* of the great drum the villagers played for three days. On the fourth day, when Annuk did not return, they took her sled dogs to the edge of the forest and set them free.

The villagers packed their belongings in their boats and rowed to an inlet far away. There they built new ice houses, and eventually everyone stopped thinking about the girl who had been snatched by the sea.

Many winters later, a solitary fisherman paddled
his kayak to the inlet where Annuk, now a skeleton,
slept under the sea, silently rocked by the currents.

The man did not know that no one ever fished in that inlet. He baited his hook, dropped his line into the water, and all day long he did not catch a single fish. As the sun stooped low in the sky, a she-wolf howled and another answered on the cliffs. The fisherman's hair stood on end.

"This place must be haunted," he thought as he hurriedly reeled in his line.

At that moment he felt such a powerful tug on his line that he was sure he had hooked a walrus or a whale. He gave a mighty heave and the sea began to toss and the waves began to froth, threatening to capsize his little boat. Although he was frightened, the man thought: "I have caught a mighty fish— perhaps the biggest in the sea."

Yet the harder he pulled the more the sea frothed and the louder the wolves howled.

When he finally brought up his catch, the fisherman saw that he had hooked no kind of fish, but a skeleton! Shaking with fear, he paddled as fast as he could toward the shore.

But Annuk was so tangled on his line that the harder the fisherman paddled, the faster she seemed to bound over the waves, chasing after his little boat.

When his kayak bumped into the sand, the man leapt out, grabbed his fishing stick, and ran for his life. But no matter how fast he ran, Annuk still chased after him, going *klakity-klak* over the snow.

At last he reached his ice house, dove in, and covered the door.

Shivering in the dark, the fisherman thought, "Finally I'm safe." He could hear the wolves barking and yelping outside. He was sure that by now they must be eating the skeleton's bones.

But when he struck a match to light his oil lamp, what did he see but Annuk's tangled bones all in a pile inside the ice house!

He turned to the door, then remembered the wolves. He stopped and took a deep breath. "They are just bones," he told himself. "They can't hurt me." So he sat on his furs and began disentangling the skeleton from his fishing line.

Gently, he set each bone where it belonged, all the time humming a song under his breath like a mother sings to a child. The fisherman wondered who the skeleton had once been and how it had ended up in the sea. He found himself feeling sorry for this person who, like him, had been alone for so long.

The fisherman worked late into the night until every whitened bone was in its place again. He then scraped the barnacles and crusty coral from her ribs. He pulled off the shreds of seaweed tangled at her head. And when he was done he covered Annuk with a warm polar-bear skin, went inside his sleeping furs, and closed his eyes. In his sleep, as he dreamed about the skeleton's lonely life under the sea, a tear ran down his cheek.

Seeing his tear, Annuk sat up quietly, so as not to awaken the fisherman. She *klakity-klakked* to his side and touched his face with hers, and felt the wetness of the tear against the hollow of her cheek.

As she bent over the fisherman, she felt the *boom boom* of his heart, like a great drum. She pressed her face to his chest and began to sing the song of life to the rhythm of his heartbeat.

*Flesh flesh flesh*
  *hands hands hands*
    mouth mouth mouth

The fisherman awoke to find a beautiful young
woman with long flowing hair and sparkling eyes
leaning over him. Annuk smiled at him, took his
hand, and led him outside. The wolf dogs began
yelping and licking Annuk's face, jumping all around
her. Her old sled dogs were now nearly wild. Over
the years their fur had turned white like the snow.

And from that day on, Annuk and the fisherman were together, living peacefully on the edge of the sea.

# AUTHOR'S NOTE

Although they are commonly referred to as Eskimos, most Arctic peoples call themselves Inuits, which means "the people." The first Inuit settled in the northernmost portions of Alaska, Greenland, Russia, and Canada during the last glacial period, nearly 30,000 years ago. They built homes of ice on the frozen tundra, where in the winter the sun never shines and in the summer it never sets.

Annuk is an Alaskan Inuit, from the Aleutian Islands chain. An Alaskan medicine woman from the Aleutian Islands told me the story of the skeleton woman, which is a legend thousands of years old. The story tells of how love can conquer all, even death.

Notes on spot illustrations:

**SUN MASK** (p. 5), **SHAMAN'S MASK** (p. 12–13), **DOUBLE KILLER WHALE MASK** (p. 16): These ceremonial masks, made of wood, are worn by medicine men and women who wish to speak directly with the spirits, such as the king of the seas—represented by the killer whale.

**SUN VISOR** (p. 20): The Inuits wear these visors to block the bright sunlight that reflects off the perpetually snow-covered ground.

**TRINKET BOX** (p. 26): Carved boxes like these are used to hold sewing needles, flints for starting fires, and other small items. This box depicts a mother seal floating with her newborn on her belly.

**SCRAPING KNIFE** (p. 29): Knives like this one are used for cleaning skins and furs. They are traditionally passed down from mother to daughter.

To Alexis, for showing me
the ways of the soul
—A. V.

To those of us who
have lost ourselves
—Y.

SIMON & SCHUSTER BOOKS FOR YOUNG READERS
An imprint of Simon & Schuster Children's Publishing Division
1230 Avenue of the Americas, New York, New York 10020
Text copyright © 1995 by Alberto Villoldo. Illustrations copyright © 1995 by Yoshi.
SIMON & SCHUSTER BOOKS FOR YOUNG READERS is a trademark of Simon & Schuster.
Book design by Paul Zakris. The text for this book is set in 16.5-point Amerigo
The illustrations were done in watercolor.
Manufactured in the United States of America
10 9 8 7 6 5 4 3 2 1

LIBRARY OF CONGRESS CATALOGING-IN-PUBLICATION DATA
Villoldo, Alberto.
Skeleton woman / by Alberto Villoldo ; illustrated by Yoshi.
p. cm.
Summary: Years after being drowned by a tsunami, Annuk is rescued
from her watery grave by the tenderness of a lonely fisherman.
1. Aleuts—Folklore. 2. Aleut women—Folklore. [1. Aleuts—Folklore. 2. Eskimos—
Folklore. 3. Folklore—Alaska—Aleutian Islands.] I. Yoshi, ill. II. Title.
E99.A34V55 1995 398.2'089971—dc20 94-49619
ISBN 0-689-80279-X